The
Hawaiian Lion

THUNDER FROM THE MOUNTAINTOP

PACIFIC

OCEAN

Kaua'i

• Lihue

Ni'ihau

O'ahu

Wahiawa •   • Kaneohe

○ **HONOLULU**

Kalaupapa   **Moloka'i**

Ho'olehua   **Wailuku**

Lana'i   Lahaina   **Maui**

Lana'i City   Lana'i   • Hana

Kaho'olawe

Kiwahu   Kiwai'i

Waimea

• Hilo

Kailua-kona

Hawai'i

N

W   E

S

Jason Louis

To Davey, Kenzo, and every child out there.
Don't be afraid to face your fears.
Have courage and never give up!

www.mascotbooks.com

The Hawaiian Lion: Thunder from the Mountaintop

©2022 Jason Louis. All Rights Reserved. No part of this
publication may be reproduced, stored in a retrieval system or
transmitted in any form by any means electronic, mechanical,
or photocopying, recording or otherwise without the
permission of the author.

For more information, please contact:
Mascot Books, an imprint of Amplify Publishing Group
620 Herndon Parkway, Suite 320
Herndon, VA 20170
info@mascotbooks.com

Library of Congress Control Number: 2022903562

CPSIA Code: PRV0822A
ISBN-13: 978-1-63755-460-9

Printed in the United States

Kimo

Elli (Elephant)

Tikki (Tiger)

Zekki (Zebra)

Raffi (Giraffe)

Mikki (Monkey)

Rikki (Rabbit)

Piggi (Pig)

Chapter One

It was a beautiful day as usual on the Hawaiian island of Kiwahu. As the morning sun peeked through the forest, Tikki Tiger and Zekki Zebra were on their way to the fruit patch on Manou Mountain.

This large fruit patch was located near the bottom of the mountain and had many fruits the animals loved to eat.

Above the fruit patch, about halfway up the mountain was a band of thick mist, and above the mist, the lush green summit.

Three times a day, for breakfast, lunch and dinner, Tikki and Zekki would visit the fruit patch. On each occasion, the village chief, Elli Elephant, would accompany them to the foot of the mountain with the same advice.

"Be careful up there. Don't go above the mist." She had a strange feeling that there was something above the mist, at the top of the mountain.

Chapter Two

From the top of the mountain, Kimo, the Hawaiian Lion, had a great view of the village below. He could see the animals making their daily trek up the hill, returning with baskets of fruits. But he never met them. Somehow, they never made it to the top.

Kimo had thoughts of having one of the animals for a meal if they came close. But that never happened. Instead, Kimo would venture down to the smaller fruit patch, just above the mist, to get his meals.

As Kimo grew older, he ate more fruit than the patch could produce.

He was getting hungrier after each meal, but he was not brave enough to go down to the village to hunt. He really loved eating fruits. They were sweet and juicy.

Kimo needed a plan since there were no fruits left in the small patch. As he sat staring at the village, he had an idea.

Chapter Three

Kimo thought to himself, *I am king of the jungle. Animals fear me. I'll let out a thunderous roar and demand that these animals bring me some of that fruit. If they don't, I will threaten to come down to the village to hunt them. I'll try that and see what happens.*

The next day, as usual, Tikki and Zekki were getting ready to visit the fruit patch for breakfast when, from the top of the mountain, came a loud roar, followed by these words:

I'M KING OF THE JUNGLE, MIGHTY AND STRONG.
BRING ME SOME BREAKFAST AND DON'T TAKE TOO LONG.
I'M HUNGRY, I'M THIRSTY, I'M STARTING TO FROWN.
YOU BETTER COME UP OR I'M COMING DOWN.

The village shook. The animals trembled.
Tikki and Zekki rushed back to the
village in fear.

The animals didn't know what to do.

"OK, calm down," said Elli, standing in the village square where all the animals had gathered. "There's something up on that mountain just as I thought all along, and it sounds like a lion."

The animals shook in fear. "A lion? Then we're all dead," they said. "What are we going to do?"

Chapter Four

"Well, we need a plan," replied Elli, "and I think I have one. Let's get the strongest animal in the village to go up the mountain to talk to the lion. If the lion does not want to talk and insists on coming down to hunt us, then our strongest will put up a fight. Who knows what might happen? I think it's worth taking a chance."

It sounded like a good plan. Elli always came up with good plans. The animals agreed. "So, who's the strongest?" she asked. All the animals pointed to Zekki.

"Why me?" Zekki cried.

"Because you are big and strong and may be our only hope," answered Elli.

Zekki accepted his fate and waved goodbye as he headed towards the mountain. Elli walked with him to the foot of the mountain. Before he started to go up, Elli gave him this advice:

"Stop at the fruit patch, pick some pineapples, and take them with you."

Chapter Five

The animals stood in silence as Zekki disappeared into the mountainside.

On the way up, he picked the finest pineapples he could find and took them with him. The animals waited and waited, and then about an hour later, a loud thunderous roar, followed by an equally loud burp, came from the mountaintop.

"Oh no! He ate Zekki!" cried the
animals. They looked at Elli and asked,
"Now what?"

"I am sorry that Zekki is no longer with us," said Elli. "But, we should count our lucky stars that the lion did not come down. It could have been worse. It's over now. Let's get back to our chores."

The animals went back to doing their daily chores, trying to forget what had happened. But there was fear in the village. At just about lunchtime, a loud and thunderous roar came from the top of the mountain again, followed by the haunting words:

I'M KING OF THE JUNGLE, MIGHTY AND STRONG.
BRING ME SOME LUNCH AND DON'T TAKE TOO LONG.
I'M HUNGRY, I'M THIRSTY, I'M STARTING TO FROWN.
YOU BETTER COME UP OR I'M COMING DOWN.

Chapter Six

The animals all rushed to the village square, shaking and trembling.

"Oh, no! Not again!" they cried. "Now what do we do?" They all looked at Elli.

"Well, let's get the fastest animal to go up the mountain this time. Perhaps he will be more successful.

"If the lion still does not want to talk and insists on coming down, then there's a chance our fastest will outrun the lion. And who knows what might happen?"

"Not a chance," replied Mikki. "We've heard that before. The next animal that goes up there will surely get eaten. Look at what happened to Zekki."

"Well, the lion's roar did not sound as strong to me. Zekki must have wounded or even weakened him," Elli said.

"It's a bad idea," said the animals.

"I think it is worth a shot," said Elli. "We have no other choice. If someone does not go up, the lion will come down." Afraid, the animals sadly agreed.

"Who is the fastest animal among us?" asked Elli. Everyone pointed to Tikki.

"Me?" squealed Tikki.

"Yes, you," said Elli. "I will walk you to the foot of the mountain."

As Elli walked with Tikki, she whispered in his ear, "Stop at the fruit patch, pick some mangoes, and take them with you."

Chapter Seven

The animals stood in silence as Tikki
disappeared into the mountainside. On
the way up, he picked the finest mangoes
he could find and took them with him.
The animals waited and waited, and
then, about an hour later, a loud roar,
followed by a loud burp, came from the
mountaintop.

"He did it again!" they cried. "First Zekki and now Tikki."

There was tension in the village. The animals were really scared now. This was a nightmare. They had no idea what to do. Looking to Elli they cried, "What will we do? This lion will keep eating us one by one until we're all gone."

Chapter Eight

"Now hold on just a minute," Elli replied. "Remember, we must have a plan."

"And what is that plan?" Rikki Rabbit shouted.

"Well, if the lion roars for his food at dinnertime, we should all go up to the mountaintop," said Elli.

"What? Are you crazy?" replied the animals. "This lion ate Zekki for breakfast and Tikki for lunch, and now you are saying we should go up there for dinner? No way."

"Calm down," replied Elli. "If we go up together, we will overpower him. He certainly can't beat us all. We will be stronger together."

That seemed to make sense to the animals. After all, it was the only chance they had of staying alive. "OK. But, who will lead the way?" they asked.

"I will," replied Elli. "Let's wait and see. If he roars again, we are going up the mountain."

Chapter Nine

The animals were too frightened to move. They remained in the village square until evening when they thought the lion would be ready for his dinner. Sure enough, at about dinnertime, a mighty roar came from the mountaintop, followed by these scary words:

"That's it. Let's go," ordered Elli.

Up the mountain the animals marched. When they got to the fruit patch, Elli stopped and said, "Let's grab some fruit to take with us."

"Fruit? Why are we taking fruit to a lion?" replied the animals. "He wants to eat us, not fruit."

"Let's try it. We have nothing to lose," said Elli. The animals each grabbed a different fruit and continued up the mountain.

Chapter Ten

As they got to the top, they smelled the lion.

"We're getting closer," warned Elli.

Peeking through the bushes, they finally saw him. He was wearing a lei and a grass skirt and looked like he was preparing a table for dinner. He seemed very happy, as he was dancing and singing the entire time.

"See," whispered the animals, "he is preparing to eat the next animal that comes up the mountain."

"Well, that's about to end right now," said Elli. "Get ready. We will take him down."

"And how do you plan to achieve that?" asked the animals.

"On the count of three, we will rush him, overpower him, and take him down. Are you ready? One, two, three!"

Just then, the lion turned around and let out a loud roar. The ground shook. The baskets fell from the paws of the animals as they trembled in fear. Elli tried her best to be brave and not shake like the other animals.

"We're all dead," squeaked Rikki Rabbit.

Chapter Eleven

The lion took one giant leap towards the animals, who were still too shocked to move. He sniffed them, smiled, and said, "Aloha! I'm Kimo. I've been waiting for you. Pick up the fruits and place them over there."

Then, with a wink, he added, "There is no need to be scared. I will not eat you. I'm only interested in fruits and wanted someone to bring me some." With that, he let out a broad smile.

The animals looked at each other, speechless. They could not believe Kimo was not interested in eating them for dinner. Relieved, they started picking up the fruits when suddenly, from the bushes, appeared Zekki and Tikki. They had not returned to the village, because they chose to spend time with Kimo on the mountaintop.

Happy to see their friends from the village, Zekki and Tikki ran to greet them.

Kimo interrupted them by inviting Elli and the animals to join him for dinner. They gladly accepted.

Chapter Twelve

After eating fruits for dinner and
listening to stories from Kimo, Elli
thought it was time to head back to the
village. But she felt bad that they were
leaving Kimo all by himself up on the
mountain.

"Why don't you come down to the village with us?" asked Elli. "I think you will like it down there, especially our large fruit patch. You will have food for life."

Kimo thought about it for a minute. "That's not a bad idea," he said. "But, with one condition: that you all wear leis with your grass skirts and dance the hula as we head down the mountain."

They all agreed. And that evening, in single file with Elli leading, they marched down the mountain wearing leis, singing, and dancing the hula.

The End

Kimo

Elli (Elephant)

Tikki (Tiger)

Zekki (Zebra)

Raffi (Giraffe)

Mikki (Monkey)

Rikki (Rabbit)

Piggi (Pig)

About the Author

Jason Louis continues to inspire the next generation of young readers with this exciting story about animals in a village facing an unexpected menace. Building on the Marco's Travels series, he combines drama, excitement, and fun in this story for kids who are ready to move on from picture books but not quite ready for full chapter books. This well-paced story, with its many twists and turns, will not disappoint.